FOURTH

FIFTH

Grace wanted to dance.

She tried.

And she tried.

And she tried.

"Give up, Grace," the other girls said.

Grace was sad.

She made a picture
and felt better.

Grace made many pictures.
Then she had an idea.

The other girls loved what Grace made.

Grace felt great.

So she kept making pictures.

She kept dancing too.

To my dad, with love; my mum, whose light shines on in me;
and with a special thanks to Ted and Betsy Lewin
for their inspiration and encouragement

I LIKE TO READ is a registered trademark of Holiday House, Inc.

Copyright © 2015 by Kate Parkinson
All Rights Reserved
HOLIDAY HOUSE is registered in the U.S. Patent and Trademark Office.
Printed and Bound in October 2014 at Toppan Leefung, DongGuan City, China.
The artwork was created with pen and ink and Photoshop.
www.holidayhouse.com
First Edition
1 3 5 7 9 10 8 6 4 2

Library of Congress Cataloging-in-Publication Data
Parkinson, Kate, author, illustrator.
Grace / by Kate Parkinson. — First edition.
pages cm. — (I like to read)
Summary: When the other girls discourage Grace from dancing,
she draws pictures to make herself feel better and succeeds
in a surprising way.
ISBN 978-0-8234-3207-3 (hardcover)
[1. Ability—Fiction. 2. Dance—Fiction. 3. Drawing—Fiction.] I. Title.
PZ7.P23933Gr 2015
[E]—dc23
2014006417

ISBN 978-0-8234-3317-9 (paperback)